D0243804

SUN

Reading Borough Council

3412601126063 8

For Amberly

A TEMPLAR BOOK

First published in the UK in 2017 by Templar Publishing,
part of the Bonnier Publishing Group,
The Plaza, 535 King's Road, London, SW10 0SZ
www.templarco.co.uk
www.bonnierpublishing.com

Copyright © 2017 by Sam Usher

1 3 5 7 9 10 8 6 4 2

All rights reserved

ISBN 978-1-78370-653-2 (Hardback)
ISBN 978-1-78370-795-9 (Paperback)

Designed by Genevieve Webster
Edited by Alison Ritchie

Printed in Malaysia

READING BOROUGH LIBRARIES	
Askews & Holts	
JF	£6.99

Sam Usher

SUN

templar publishing

When I woke up
this morning,
it was sunny.

It was the hottest day
of the year.

I said, "It's hotter than broccoli soup,

hotter than the Atacama Desert,

and hotter than the surface of the sun."

Grandad said, "It's the perfect day
for an adventure."

So we gathered our necessary provisions.

I was lookout and Grandad was navigator.

He said, "Let's find the perfect picnic spot."

The sun beat down.

Grandad said,
"Let's have a rest."
And I said,
"What are we
looking for, Grandad?"
And he said,
"Somewhere picturesque."

So Grandad navigated and I looked out.

And I said, "What about this way, Grandad?"

The sun beat down.

Grandad said,
"Let's have a rest."
And I said,
"What are we
looking for, Grandad?"
And he said,
"Somewhere in the shade."

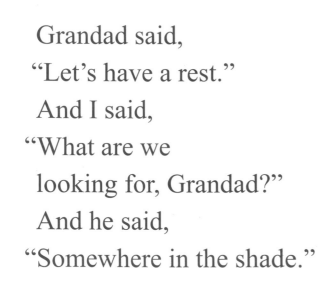

So Grandad navigated and I looked out.

And I said, "What about this way, Grandad?"

We walked for miles.

Grandad said, "Let's have a rest."
And I said, "What are we
looking for, Grandad?"
And he said,
"Somewhere
with a cool
breeze."

So Grandad navigated and I looked out.

And I said, "What about this way, Grandad?"

The sun beat down.

I said, "Look, Grandad,
what about over there?"

But someone had got there first.

So we helped
them gather
their provisions.

And we
shared
the perfect
picnic
spot.

Back at home,
Grandad said,
"If you keep looking,
you never know
what you might find."

And I agreed.

I hope it's sunny
again tomorrow.